CHILL OUT SCOOBY-DOO!

SCHOLASTIC INC.

New York Toronto London Auckland Sydney
Mexico City New Delhi Hong Kong Buenos Aires

ISBN-13: 978-0-439-91595-3
ISBN-10: 0-439-91595-3

Designed by Michael Massen

12 11 10 9 8 7 6 5 4 3 2 1   7 8 9 10 11/0

Printed in the U.S.A.

First printing, August 2007

INTRODUCTION

Climbing inch by inch, two men made their way up a steep, snowy cliff. They were on Mount Everest, the world's tallest peak. A rope tied them together for safety.

In the lead was a mountain guide named Pemba. He looked down at the man below him. "We must keep climbing, Professor!" he called. "It is not far now!"

Below him, Professor Robinson Jeffries clung to the mountainside, breathing heavily. "Yes, of course," he replied, panting. "Just need to . . . catch my breath."

While Professor Jeffries rested, Pemba climbed a little higher. He reached a rocky ridge and looked over it. His eyes went wide as he stared in awe at what he saw.

A large, flat stone slab stood on the ridge. Pictures and symbols were carved into it. "There it is," he shouted down to the professor, "just as I have promised you!"

Professor Jeffries was suddenly filled with new energy. He hurried up the mountain to join Pemba. He, too, was amazed at what he saw. "So, the legend is true!" he cried excitedly. Laughing with delight, he continued, "I've found it at last! Come, Pemba! The lost kingdom of Shangri-La must be just ahead!"

The professor began to climb, but Pemba wouldn't budge. "I'm sorry, Professor, but we dare not go further. These lands are forbidden!"

Professor Jeffries chuckled. "Forbidden? By whom? We're the only ones here!"

"No. We are not alone," Pemba said, pointing to huge footprints in the snow. The wind began to howl. Snow swirled around them. "We should not be here!" Pemba went on, his voice quaking in fear. "He is coming."

Professor Jeffries took out a knife and cut the rope that connected them. "Then I'll go alone," he insisted.

The wind howled. Snow came down hard. Pemba could no longer see the professor because of the blizzard. "Professor!" he called. "Professor!"

Suddenly, a gigantic, hairy figure stepped out of the blinding snow. It towered over Pemba, roaring.

Pemba stumbled backward, terrified. His foot went over the edge, and he tumbled off the narrow ridge. Thinking fast, he grabbed his axe from his belt and smashed it into the side of the mountain. It held! As he dangled helplessly, he didn't dare look down at the 10,000-foot drop below him.

Another roar filled the cold air. Looking up, Pemba saw the creature climb up the steep mountain wall above him with great ease. And then he was gone!

Pemba gasped. "*I have seen it,*" he thought in amazement, "*the Abominable Snowman!*"

Chapter

Shaggy Rogers and Scooby-Doo, his Great Dane and best pal, were enjoying themselves. "What a great idea, Scoob," Shaggy said, his mouth stuffed with pizza. "Like, I've always wanted to fly on an all-you-can-eat airline."

Scooby-Doo crammed three slices in his mouth at once. "Reah, ree, too!" he agreed.

"But, like, gee whiz! Shouldn't we have landed in Paris by now?" he wondered. Shaggy and Scooby were on their way to meet the rest of the Gang in Paris for a vacation. Scooby-Doo and Shaggy had insisted on flying separately on this special all-you-can-eat flight. They had hardly noticed that there were no other passengers.

Scooby-Doo looked out the window. He was shocked by what he saw. Those high snow-covered mountains didn't look like they were anywhere near Paris!

In the plane's cockpit, Alphonse LeFleur sat beside the pilot. He was a French-Canadian trapper with a wild, crazy look in his eyes. He grinned as they flew above the mountains. "Aha! Mount Everest—home of the Abominable Snowman. I am Alphonse LeFleur, the world's greatest monster hunter! Now I come in search of the world's greatest prize!"

"So what are you using for bait?" the pilot asked.

"I have bait no monster can resist!" Alphonse LeFleur replied. Just then a light on the plane's control panel flashed. LeFleur was annoyed. "What could they want now?" he grumbled as he got out of his seat.

He walked into the cabin where Scooby-Doo and Shaggy were sitting. Pizza boxes were piled to the ceiling beside them. Alphonse LeFleur forced himself to smile. "*Bon jour, mes amis!*" he greeted them. "And thank you for flying Alphonse LeFleur's Le Monde Grande Tours. We will be landing shortly."

"Boy, are we glad to hear that!" Shaggy told him. "Like, my stomach is already coming in for a three-snack landing."

"Not to worry," LeFleur said. "We have lots of yummy goodies waiting for you in our lounge. Come with me."

Scooby and Shaggy eagerly followed him to the back of the plane toward a large crate surrounded by camping gear. When Scooby-Doo noticed the box of Scooby Snacks inside the crate, he dove right in. Shaggy was right behind.

As soon as they were inside, Alphonse LeFleur sealed the crate and pushed it out of the plane! "Elevator going down!" Shaggy cried as the box tumbled over and over, falling faster through the air, with Scooby and Shaggy crammed inside.

Scooby-Doo whimpered in fear.

"You said it, Scoob!" Shaggy agreed. "Like, I think we've just been bumped from first class to worst class!"

Above them, the parachute attached to the crate opened, and the box stopped turning and began to fall more slowly. Something in the box began to ring. "Great! Now my ears are ringing!" Shaggy wailed.

Scooby-Doo moved his paw as best he could. "Rell phone! Rell phone!" he said, trying to point to Shaggy's ringing cell phone.

Shaggy's face lit into a smile. "Like, way to go, Scoob! It must be the Gang!" Shaggy inched the phone out of his back pocket and answered it, "Like, world's worst vacation EVER! Shaggy speaking."

Fred was on the other end. "Shaggy! Where are you guys?"

Peeking their heads out of an opening in the crate, they peered down at the icy mountains below. "We don't know, but like, think of the frostiest, frozen-est place you've ever been to and then times that by a hundred," Shaggy reported, as they moved their heads back into the crate.

A terrible sound filled the crate. It was the sound of something ripping. "Like, hang on, Freddie," Shaggy said, his voice quaking. He stuck his head back out to check.

One of the ropes holding their parachute had

broken! The crate now hung sideways, fastened to only one rope. It began to fall more quickly.

"Guys, are you okay?" Fred shouted into the phone. "What's happening?"

Shaggy ducked down into the swiftly falling crate. He was about to answer Fred when another big ripping sound came from above.

This time the crate fell completely loose and plummeted end over end toward the mountains below.

Shaggy clutched the cell phone to the side of his face. "Like, I think Scoob and I are about to go from frequent fliers to frequent criers!" he shouted to Fred.

But the only answer was static on the phone.

Chapter 2

Daphne, Velma, and Fred sat at a table in a French café in Paris. They could see the Eiffel Tower just in front of them. But at the moment, Velma and Daphne were too busy watching Fred speak on his fancy new cell phone to enjoy the view.

He put down the cell phone, frowning. "I've lost their signal. I think they're in some kind of trouble."

"Can't you trace them with that high-tech GPS thingy that came on your new phone?" Daphne asked.

"That's right, Daphne!" he exclaimed. "With this Global Positioning System, I should be able to pinpoint their exact location." Fred turned to his cell phone and pushed several buttons. He found them. "But wait!" he cried, confused. "That can't be right!"

Daphne and Velma leaned over to see what the GPS was telling Fred. "The Himalayas!" they both shouted at the same time.

Velma picked up one of the French newspapers she had been reading. "Listen to this, Gang!" she said. "It says here that climbers on Mount Everest claim to have seen the Abominable Snowman, a mysterious creature believed to exist in the high Himalayas!"

Velma and Fred were instantly on their feet, but Daphne grabbed hold of them, pulling them back into their seats. "Now hold on! Just because there's a monster on the loose doesn't necessarily mean that Shaggy and Scooby are going to get into trouble . . . does it?"

Daphne didn't even wait for them to answer. If there was trouble, Scooby-Doo and Shaggy were ALWAYS in the thick of it! In the next second they were all running for their van, the Mystery Machine.

"We've got to get to Mount Everest!" Fred said as he turned on the van and began to drive.

Daphne sighed. "Ooh, just once I'd like to have a vacation that stayed a vacation!"

The Gang drove for days over many miles, going east toward Mongolia. Fred's GPS tracking device had done a great job of helping them find their way. But at the moment they weren't all that sure where they were. They didn't even seem to be on a real road.

As they drove, Velma told them what she knew about the Abominable Snowman. "There are a number of different theories regarding the creature," she said. "Some believe it to be a lost tribe of early cave people somehow surviving through the ages in the high mountains. It could also be a *Gigantopithecus*, the largest mountain gorilla that ever existed. But, according to records, these large primates have been extinct for over a hundred thousand years."

She pulled out a photo printed from the online research she'd done on her laptop computer. It was of a giant footprint. "There have been many sightings, and many photos have been taken of Yeti's footprints."

"Hold it," Daphne said. "Back up. *What* on Earth is a Yeti?"

"Yeti is the name used by the local mountain people to describe the creature," Velma replied.

"Well, if it's out there," Fred said, "I'm sure Shaggy and Scooby-Doo will find it."

Chapter

3

High in the mountains, on the long, steep steps of an ancient monastery, Professor Jeffries met Pemba once again. He told the guide how he'd wandered in the blizzard for hours before finding his way to the village just below the monastery. It was the same village where Pemba lived with his family. "It's my own fault," Pemba said. "I should never have taken you as far as the forbidden lands."

"But you did, Pemba!" the professor insisted. "And the discovery of a lifetime is still within our grasp! The lost kingdom of Shangri-La is up there just waiting for us."

"But the Yeti is guarding the lost city," Pemba reminded him. "That's why everyone is fleeing the village."

A girl of about eighteen came toward them. She wore the traditional dress of her village but had on headphones which were attached to a radio hanging from her shoulder. She carried a tray with two cups of tea on it. "Minga! What are you doing here?" Pemba scolded, lifting the headphones off her ears. "You should be leaving with the others!"

"I'm not scared of your snowman stories anymore," she argued. "I'm not a little girl anymore."

"Please excuse my sister, Professor Jeffries," Pemba said. "She is as stubborn as a yak."

At that moment, Minga, Pemba, and Professor Jeffries all turned to see something zooming down the mountainside and heading straight for them. The dilapidated crate carried two figures who were screaming in complete panic.

It was Shaggy and Scooby-Doo!

"We may be freezing cold, but we're coming in hot!" Shaggy shouted. They hit a snow ledge and sailed into the air. Flying over the heads of Pemba, Minga, and Professor Jeffries, they smashed through the monastery wall, landing inside.

"Egads! Are you all right?" Professor Jeffries called out as the three of them ran up the steps to Scooby-Doo and Shaggy. "Did you break anything?"

Shaggy stood and weaved in a shaky circle. "Like, only the land-speed record for freestyle toboggan!" he joked.

"Ruh-huh," Scooby-Doo agreed, nodding weakly.

Minga giggled. "They're funny."

The High Lama, the head of the monastery, appeared in a balcony and angrily demanded to know what had happened. When Pemba explained that the two friends had fallen from the sky, the lama became more welcoming, thinking that Scooby-Doo and Shaggy were mystical beings. "Do you mind if we use your phone?" Shaggy requested.

"I am sorry," the lama told them. "We have no such modern things here. Life at the monastery has not changed in thousands of years." He took them all on a tour of the monastery where they saw a chamber filled with frightening carvings of the Abominable Snowman.

"Holy smokes!" Shaggy remarked nervously. "Who does your decorating in here — Dracula?"

"In this chamber we offer sacrifices to the

Yeti, the creature also known as the Abominable Snowman," the lama explained. "Half man, half animal, he lives in the snow caves high in the mountains."

In the chamber was an altar. At its center was a brilliantly shining centerpiece, a glowing crystal. "This is our most sacred item," the High Lama explained. "It is a gift from the ancient ones of the mountains."

Professor Jeffries was amazed by the crystal. "May I examine it more closely?" he asked the High Lama.

"No! You may not!" the lama snapped. "The crystal is sacred! Its mystical glow protects us from the creature's evil power."

Suddenly, Alphonse LeFleur burst into the chamber.

"Zoinks!" Shaggy shouted. "Look out, Scoob! It's that terrible tour guide!"

"My sincerest apologies," LeFleur told them. "There was a terrible mishap. I was so worried that I jumped out of the plane to save you."

"Speaking of saving us," Shaggy said. "The rest of the Gang must be worried sick about us." Minga suggested that they try calling the Gang from the weather station further up the mountain where there was a satellite hookup.

Pemba agreed to take them there. Professor Jeffries and Alphonse LeFleur insisted on coming along as well. Minga begged to go, too, but Pemba refused, ordering her to leave the village along with the other villagers.

They suited up in thermal gear, took sleds loaded with supplies, and began climbing. Before long, Shaggy felt the need for a little snack and began to search around the sleds. He pulled back a tarp and found boxes marked DANGER and SCIENTIFIC EQUIPMENT. "Don't touch that!" Professor Jeffries scolded harshly.

Shaggy jumped back.

"I'm sorry," the professor apologized, "but this equipment is very sensitive."

Shaggy and Scooby were the slowest climbers and soon fell to the back of the group. Soon, they had the feeling that they were being followed.

The group discovered it was Minga who was following, trekking along behind them. She had been there all along.

Pemba was angry with her for not leaving the

village with the others as he had told her to. "There's bad weather coming," Minga said, defending her actions. "I came to warn you."

"You came along because you have a crush on the weatherman who pretends he's also a dee-jay," Pemba disagreed. "What is his name? Yes, I recall, Del Chillman."

"Del Chillman!" Shaggy cried. "Like, Scoob and I know the guy! We met him when we uncovered the case of the Loch Ness Monster over in Scotland."

"Well, my sister has a huge crush on his radio voice. She has made up this whole story about a storm just so she can come with us and meet him," Pemba said.

"That's not true!" Minga argued. "Del Chillman is leaving the weather station soon. He said so himself on the radio. So why should I bother having a crush on someone who is going away soon? Besides — there *is* a storm coming!"

In the distance, they saw a black mass of swirling snow coming toward them. They decided it was best to seek shelter from the storm while there was still time to set up their tents.

Shaggy and Scooby-Doo crawled into their tent just as the last rays of daylight disappeared. "That psychotic snowman is out there on the loose," Shaggy worried.

As he spoke, a terrible roar filled the snowy night air.

Alphonse LeFleur leaped out of his tent holding an elephant gun. "The creature! He knows we are here!"

The roar came again — closer and scarier this time.

"Zoinks!" Shaggy squealed. "And he doesn't sound too happy about it."

"Do not worry, my friends," said Alphonse LeFleur. "My traps are set."

"Zoinks! Like, I get it now," Shaggy cried. "You're not really a tour guide."

"No, my friend! I am Alphonse LeFleur, the greatest monster hunter in the world!"

Suddenly, Shaggy realized something that made him shake. "And we're just monster bait to help you catch that cold cretin!"

Alphonse LeFleur shrugged and nodded. "What can I say? I read the newspaper story about the teenaged gang and the big dog, Scooby-Doo, and how the monsters, they chase them everywhere they go."

Shaggy and Scooby-Doo frowned and grumbled. But a third roar made them jump together, clutching one another with terror! The monster was right there on a nearby ridge, outlined in moonlight.

"The monster, it is here!" Alphonse LeFleur shouted excitedly.

"And like, we're gone man!" Shaggy told him as he and Scooby-Doo began to run. "Like, *reeeaaal* gone! Grab the Scooby Snacks, Scoob. We're outta here!"

Chapter

The next morning, Fred, Velma, and Daphne trudged up the snowy mountainside searching for Shaggy and Scooby-Doo. Fred's GPS had guided them as far as the monastery. "Jeepers! What happened here?" Daphne wondered. All the tents had been torn to pieces.

"Look around you," Velma said. The Gang turned. Giant footsteps were everywhere.

"They must belong to the Abominable Snowman!" Fred said.

"Look closer," Velma told them as she crouched down to study the prints. "The creature's footprint, while larger in size, only sinks half as deep into the snow as Daphne's."

"That doesn't make sense. How could I weigh more than a snow monster?" Daphne asked.

A groaning sound made them stand still and listen. "Over here!" Fred shouted, running toward a large cage. Inside, they found Pemba, nearly frozen.

After they'd warmed him with blankets and made him some hot tea on the camp stove, Pemba told the Gang what had happened. The Abominable Snowman had lifted him up and stuffed him into the cage that they'd brought along to capture the monster. Afterward, he'd ripped the camp apart. Pemba didn't know what had happened to the others.

The Gang began looking closely at the big footprints. "From the looks of these, I'd say Professor Jeffries sneaked away alone," Velma said. "His prints are lightly snow-covered and seem to have been made before the others."

"But why go climbing alone at night in the middle of a snowstorm?" Daphne wondered.

"And check this out!" Fred said, showing them the area around Alphonse LeFleur's tent. All sorts of traps had been set up — laser trip wires, magnetic snares, collapsing bolt springs! "Man, this guy is good!" Fred remarked.

"Not good enough to stop the monster last night," Velma pointed out.

"I don't see my sister Minga's footprints here," Pemba said.

"I wonder if that means the monster carried her away," Velma said softly to herself. She followed the trail of huge monster footprints up a path. She stopped when she saw something lying in the snow. "Jinkies! Look! It's a radio!"

The others came running. "It's Minga's!" Pemba cried unhappily. "She never goes anywhere without it!"

"She must have dropped it as the snowman carried her away," Velma said seriously.

"And what about Shaggy and Scooby?" Fred asked. "They must still be out there somewhere."

Daphne threw her arms out helplessly at her sides, worried sick about her pals. "Oh, Scooby-Doo . . . where are you?" she called. Suddenly, as if in answer to Daphne's question, Minga's radio came to life. *Rooby-rooby-roo!*

Then Shaggy's voice came on! He was laughing! "That's right, old buddy!" Shaggy said.

"I don't believe it!" Daphne cried out. "It's Scooby and Shaggy! And they're on the radio!"

They all crowded around the radio to listen.

"And now for all you mountain music lovers, it's time for your mid-morning traffic report," Shaggy's voice came from the radio. "There's a six-yak pileup on the Tibetan Tri-level, and the Bhutan Expressway is a parking lot all the way to Katmandu."

"He's doing the traffic report?" Fred said, amazed. "I guess that proves they made it to the weather station. I wonder what happened to the weatherman, though."

"Hold on, folks," Shaggy continued to report over the radio. "My sidekick, Mr. Scooby, has just handed me a note. Let me read it."

There was a pause . . . and then they heard Shaggy squeal with terror! "Zoinks! Ladies and gentlemen, we interrupt our regularly sched- uled program to bring you this special report, like, live as it happens . . . the Abominable Snowman is right outside our weather station tent! Like, HEELLLPPPPP!"

Sounds of smashing and crashing came over the radio. Then all they heard was static. "Jinkies! They've gone off the air!" Velma gasped.

"We've got to get to that weather sta- tion — and fast!" Fred said.

Scooby and Shaggy were headed to Paris to meet up with the rest of the Mystery, Inc. Gang, but there was a problem . . .

Scooby and Shaggy got on the wrong airplane and ended up in the Himalayas, home to the legendary Abominable Snowman.

Scooby and Shaggy dropped in on Professor Jeffries who was searching for the lost city of Shangri-La, with Pemba, his guide, and Minga, Pemba's sister. Minga never went anywhere without her radio – she loved DJ Del Chillman!

Shaggy and Scooby, the Abominable Snowman dropped in on them!

Radio DJ Del Chillman came to the rescue. "I came here months ago in search of the Yeti, but never saw him," said Del. "But now that I'm about to leave the mountain, the tracks are everywhere!"

Del Chillman took Scooby and Shaggy back to the radio station to warm up and showed them the strange fan mail he had gotten.

DEAR DEL,
THANK YOU FOR
PLAYING SUCH
GREAT MUSIC.
PLEASE DON'T
LEAVE THE
MOUNTAIN.
I LOVE ALWAYS!
YOUR #1 FAN.

ON AIR

Soon the rest of the gang arrived to help Shaggy and Scooby. They found their friends campsite, but it looked like the Yeti had beaten them there.

Shaggy had found their way into the lost kingdom of Shangri-La.

The rest of the gang, Del Chillman, and Pemba met up with Scooby and Shaggy in an underground cave. That's where they found Professor Jeffries stealing precious crystals. "Let's make a plan to catch this crystal craving creep!" said Fred.

The professor chased Scooby and Shaggy, who had stolen his sacred crystal, and the Yeti chased the professor.

Scooby and Shaggy got out of the way and the professor and the Yeti tumbled into the gates of the monastery.

Just then an avalanche came crashing down toward Del and Velma. Suddenly, the Abominable Snowman came to the rescue!

This snowman was a snow *woman!* It was Minga, Del's biggest fan. She brought the legend of the Yeti to life hoping that it would keep him on the mountain!

"That's real cool mama," said Del.

"Scooby-Dooby-Doo!" said Scooby-Doo.

"You go," Pemba told them. "I must search for Minga up there in the monster's cave."

"Pemba's right," Fred agreed. "We should split up. Daphne, you and I will head over to the weather station."

"No, I think I should go with Pemba since I love to mountain climb," Daphne disagreed. "You and Velma go to the weather station."

"All right, Gang," Fred said. "Let's just hope we can solve this mystery before Shaggy and Scooby wind up in a deep freeze."

Chapter

Scooby-Doo and Shaggy climbed up the high radio tower, hoping the Abominable Snowman wouldn't be able to reach them. But when they were nearly to the top, they saw him climbing up the other side after them. "We're trapped, Scoob!" Shaggy wailed. "Our goose is cooked. Our egg is boiled. Our tofu is fully fricasseed."

They stared at one another unsure of what to do next. "HELLPP!!" they yelled.

The snowman was right below them. Its giant, hairy hand reached up, but at that very moment, a huge net fell over the monster. The net came from a large helium balloon that floated beside the tower. There was a man on top of the balloon, grinning. "Alphonse LeFleur!" Shaggy said, laughing with relief. "What took you so long?"

Before Alphonse LeFleur could reply, the

snowman ripped through the net! Reaching forward, he yanked on the balloon and hurled it downward onto the ice below.

Alphonse LeFleur skidded along, about to go over a cliff. Just in time, he dug into the ground with his ice axe, stopping his slide. Getting to his feet, he took out a rifle and aimed it at the Abominable Snowman.

The snowman leaped off the tower and came after him, roaring. Afraid, Alphonse LeFleur fired his rifle into the air.

The monster's roar and the sound of the fired rifle caused the ice under Alphonse LeFleur's feet to crack! The monster jumped back onto the tower. But Alphonse LeFleur fell backward off the cliff.

"He's gone!" Shaggy gasped.

The Abominable Snowman climbed toward Scooby-Doo and Shaggy once again. Shaggy noticed another weather balloon tied to the tower. He turned a nearby helium valve, and the balloon grew bigger and bigger. Soon it was big enough for Scooby-Doo to jump onto. Shaggy grabbed his tail and hung on tight.

For several terrifying moments, Shaggy swung

in the air clutching onto Scooby's tail, as the monster batted at them. When Shaggy saw the chance, he used his ice axe to cut the rope. Just as the snowman was about to get them, they sailed skyward into the open air.

Once they had left the Abominable Snowman behind, they began wondering how to get down. Scooby-Doo tried turning one of the balloon's helium valves. He wanted to open the valve just enough to let out some helium to lower the balloon, but he opened the valve too far and helium came rushing out.

The balloon shot out of control, whipping them over the tops of the mountains. At last, the balloon ran out of helium and came to a sputtering halt.

"Don't look now, Scoob, but I think our stock is about to take a serious plunge!" said Shaggy.

Shaggy and Scooby screamed as they plummeted to the ground.

They fell right into a snowbank. One after the other, their heads popped out of the snow. "That wasn't so bad after all," Shaggy said with a smile.

But his grin faded as he gazed around. They were in a spooky-looking place full of jagged rocks. Ravens sat atop the rocks, cawing at them. "Zoinks! Like, what kind of creepy place is this?" Shaggy wondered.

Growling came from somewhere nearby. Glowing eyes were all around them.

"Hey, we're in luck, Scoob!" Shaggy joked, as the eyes came close enough for him to tell what they belonged to. "It's a pack of very hungry white wolves."

Scooby-Doo and Shaggy shook with fear and clutched each other tightly while they waited for the wolves to tear them apart. But the wolves suddenly whimpered and ran away. "Hey, like, what's with them?" Shaggy asked.

A blinding light rose up from behind a nearby bank of snow. The High Lama they had met back at the monastery suddenly appeared. In his hand he held the bright crystal he'd shown them at the monastery. He waved his hand over it and its glowing light faded. "I am wondering . . . what are you doing here among the gravestones of the spirits?" he asked them.

"G-g-g-gravestones!" Shaggy yelped. He and Scooby-Doo scrambled in midair and hid behind the lama.

"Fear not, honored ones," the High Lama told them. He beckoned for them to follow him over a steep, rocky bridge with a rushing river far beneath it. On the other side of the bridge was an ancient building. There were green forests surrounding it and no snow anywhere in sight. "Welcome, honored ones, to the lost kingdom of Shangri-La," the lama explained.

"Uh . . . pardon me, your High Lamaness," Shaggy spoke up. "But, like, what happened to this place?"

"Many years ago, men came from the outside world, driven by greed," he replied. "Paradise was lost."

"Hey, that must be why the Abominable Snowman has such a chilly personality. Like, maybe he's been trying to protect this place from the outside world," Shaggy figured.

"You are very wise," the lama praised him. "Come. I will show you to your chambers. You may stay as long as you wish."

The lush jungle was alive with tropical sounds as Scooby-Doo and Shaggy followed the High Lama through the tall doors leading into Shangri-La. "You know, Scoob," Shaggy said. "I could get used to a place like this."

"Re, too," Scooby-Doo agreed.

Chapter 6

Several hours later, Fred and Velma reached the weather station. They got there just as Del Chillman returned on his snowmobile. "Fred? Velma? Man, I thought you guys were in Paris," he greeted them.

"Del?" Fred asked, surprised to see the man they had met on their Loch Ness Monster case.

"Yeah. Surprised? I gave up looking for the Loch Ness Monster because it never showed up," he explained. "So I came up here thinking I could get a look at the Abominable Snowman instead. I never saw him, either. So I planned to leave. I even announced that I was leaving over the radio. And then — would you believe it? — the Abominable Snowman suddenly showed up." Del stared at the torn weather station tent. "It looks like he was here while I was out," he added unhappily.

"He sure was," Velma agreed, showing him the big footprints around the station. "We heard him attacking Scooby-Doo and Shaggy over the radio. How did they get on the radio, anyway?"

"I asked them to fill in for me while I went out looking for survivors of the storm," Del told Fred and Velma as they followed him into his wrecked weather station. "They came up here to try to call you guys, but my satellite connection was blocked by the heavy snows. They said they'd been running from the monster, and I guess it followed them up here."

Velma began flipping through a large inventory book. "Maybe there was something else here that the snowman was after, besides Scooby and Shaggy," she said. "According to these inventory records, a few of your helium tanks are missing."

"We use helium to fill our weather balloons. But . . . they're missing?" Del replied.

"What would a snow creature want with pressurized helium?" Velma wondered.

BANG! Their talk was interrupted by a loud explosion.

Fred, Velma, and Del raced outside. A section of the mountainside had been blown away. "The explosion must have done this!" Fred said.

Looking down the mountainside, they saw a stone bridge below. It connected one underground cave with another. "It's probably been down there for centuries," Velma said. "It's just been covered with snow all this time."

"If we could only find some way down there," Fred said.

Del ran behind the weather station and returned with climbing equipment. He strapped himself into a harness and rope. "Strap in," he told them. "If there's a chance Scooby and Shaggy are in there, we're going down."

Fred and Velma strapped into harnesses and followed Del to the icy bridge. They walked carefully along the crumbling walkway. If they slipped, they would have fallen many miles onto sheets of ice.

They came to the opening of one of the caves. Inside they found strange carvings on the rock walls. Ancient pillars stood in rows, falling down and half ruined. "Whoa! What is this freaky place?" Del wondered.

Fred boldly walked farther into the cave. "Come on, Gang. It's time to put this mystery on ice," he said.

Chapter 7

Inside Shangri-La, the High Lama left Scooby-Doo and Shaggy alone to enjoy the ancient art gallery. Creeping along the dimly lit passage, they shivered. The paintings and sculptures showed wild-haired demons with fire spurting from their mouths and other scary scenes. Shaggy made jokes about how ugly the creatures in the paintings looked.

When they turned one corner, they came to a gigantic statue of the Abominable Snowman. "Now this guy is the ugliest of them all," Shaggy told Scooby-Doo, giggling.

"He's so ugly he has to sneak up on himself in the mirror," Shaggy went on, laughing even harder.

Suddenly the statue roared, shaking the other paintings.

He was no statue! He was the real thing!

"Zoinks! It's the Abominable Snowman!" Shaggy shouted. "And I don't think he appreciates my honesty!"

Scooby-Doo and Shaggy took off running, with the snowman racing behind them. He chased them up and down winding hallways, his hot breath growing ever warmer on their necks. Just when he seemed about to grab them — Scooby-Doo and Shaggy spied an escape hatch.

It was a small elevator! They jumped in and quickly unwound the rope that raised and lowered the creaky elevator. But their weight was too much for the contraption to bear and the rope snapped.

Scooby and Shaggy screamed as the elevator plummeted into the darkness. It landed with a *bang!* Scooby and Shaggy looked around. They were in a dark cavern with many tunnels leading into it.

They climbed out of the elevator and began to creep along one of the dark, spooky tunnels. They came to a corner where three tunnels met and suddenly they heard voices.

Someone was calling their names.

It sounded like Fred!

It was! Velma and Del were right behind him. The three of them cried out happily when they saw Scooby-Doo and Shaggy.

"Scooby! Shaggy! Thank goodness you're alive!" Velma shouted.

They heard someone running toward them from the other tunnel. Daphne and Pemba stepped out of the darkness! They explained that they'd been searching for Minga in the cave and had gotten lost.

They had also heard the blasts. "They seem to be coming from underground," Daphne observed.

"We must leave," Pemba warned. "This cave could collapse at any moment."

Just then, another blast rocked the cave. Stone and dirt rained down on them. Crying out in terror, the Gang and their friends ran to escape the cave-in. They stopped when they came out on a ledge. Below them was a glittering mine. "Wow!" Fred cried. "It's some kind of crystal cave!"

"Look! There's somebody down there!" Daphne said. She pointed at a figure crouching near a giant crystal. He had a sled full of equipment and carts loaded to the brim with shining crystals. It was Professor Jeffries! "I should have known it!" Pemba said. "Professor Jeffries is trying to steal the sacred crystals."

The professor had a sled loaded with dynamite. A stack of the explosive sticks was several yards away from him. He sat behind a detonator box, about to push down on the controls to set off another blast. He was the one creating the explosions!

BANG! BOOM!

The professor pressed the controls button, and the cave shook with exploding dynamite. It nearly knocked the Gang and their pals off the ledge. Crystals broke loose from the cave walls. Before the dust even settled, the professor hurried to gather up as many crystals as he could.

"One more explosion like that and this cavern will collapse," Velma said.

"Come on, Gang," Fred said. "I have a plan to catch this crystal-craving creep."

Creeping toward Professor Jeffries, Scooby-Doo and Shaggy reached the mining cart filled with crystals. Silently, they snuck off with it. They'd gone several yards when Professor Jeffries saw Scooby-Doo and Shaggy dragging it away. "Why you!" he bellowed. "Come back here with that!"

He chased Scooby-Doo and Shaggy, running after the cart.

"Hit it, guys," Fred instructed from the ledge of the rock wall above.

Del and Pemba shoved a sled filled with rocks over the side of the ledge. The sled was attached to a net made of climbing rope. The rope ran through a series of hooks and pulleys. It landed on Professor Jeffries, gathering him up!

Everyone ran to the trapped professor. "Now that's a classic example of how to trap a would-be snow monster," Daphne said.

"No! You've got it all wrong!" Professor Jeffries cried angrily as the Gang unwrapped the net. "I'm not the snow monster. This cave is what the monster has been protecting all along. There are enough riches here for all of us. Just fill your pockets!"

A terrible roar filled the cave.

The Abominable Snowman had returned!

Del and Pemba ran to an empty mining cart and got in. Daphne, Velma, and Fred hopped in with them. Scooby-Doo and Shaggy were still attached to the cart full of crystals. Running as fast as they could, dragging the cart behind them, they disappeared down a tunnel.

The Abominable Snowman leaped on top of the cart filled with the rest of the dynamite. With a strong shove, the monster set the cart rolling along a track after the Gang and their friends.

Professor Jeffries jumped into another cart. He headed down the track after Shaggy and Scooby-Doo. He was determined to get his crystals back!

Scooby-Doo and Shaggy swooped around turns and sped down steep passageways. Professor Jeffries was after them — and so was the Abominable Snowman! The snowman had forgotten about the others. Now he leaped from cart to cart trying to get to Shaggy, Scooby-Doo, and the crystals. Professor Jeffries also leaped from one cart to the next.

Scooby-Doo and Shaggy unhooked themselves from their cart and sprung from cart to cart, too. Soon they found themselves in the cart with the dynamite.

Professor Jeffries jumped onto the crystal cart. "The crystal is mine!" Professor Jeffries shouted happily as he sat on top of the shining gems.

"You can have them!" Shaggy shouted to him. "And they come with an extra bonus," he added as the monster leaped onto the crystal cart. "An Abominable Snowman!"

Shaggy and Scooby-Doo rolled away on the dynamite cart and traveled into a pitch-black tunnel. "Like, I can't see a thing, Scoob," Shaggy said. "Why don't you light a candle?"

Scooby-Doo scooped up something that felt like a candle. He lit it with a match from the box he found on the cart.

But it wasn't a candle, it was a stick of dynamite!

Terrified, Scooby and Shaggy juggled the dynamite back and forth frantically. Shaggy fumbled it, and the stick landed near the other dynamite, lighting all the fuses.

Their cart was now a speeding bomb.

Just then, Professor Jeffries's cart containing the monster and the crystals rolled up behind them. It came close enough that Scooby-Doo and Shaggy could leap onto it.

The slope of the track reversed unexpectedly. The cart with Scooby-Doo, Shaggy, the professor, and the Abominable Snowman was now in the lead — and it was being chased downhill by the cart filled with bombs!

Chapter

8

A mining cart hurtled out of a cave. Inside were Fred, Daphne, Velma, Pemba, and Del. With a crash, it fell down onto the side of an icy mountain slope. "This is going to hurt!" Del shouted as the cart slid bumpily for a long time before settling into a snowbank.

"I was right," he said when they had completely stopped. "That hurt."

"Shaggy and Scooby must still be inside the mountain somewhere," Velma said, looking around for them.

Fred climbed out of the cart. He spied Del's snowmobile a little way off. It gave him an idea. "All right, Gang. I have a plan to catch this freezer-burned bogeyman," he said. "We're going to have to move fast. Del and Velma, you're going to drive."

* * *

Del and Velma drove the snowcat around the mountain near to where the cave let out. They turned sharply and dug smooth pathways into the snow. "Way to go, guys," Fred spoke to them through his walkie-talkie. He and Daphne were higher up the cliff watching through binoculars. "The slope looks sweet," he said. "And just in time. Here they come!"

Scooby-Doo, Shaggy, Professor Jeffries, and the snowman hurtled out of the cave's mouth, just as the Gang and their friends had done. The bomb cart flew out right behind them.

KABOOM!

The bomb cart exploded in the air. The professor, the monster, Scooby-Doo, and Shaggy were thrown from the cart just seconds before it was blown to pieces!

As they flew through the air, Scooby-Doo grabbed a piece of the broken cart. "Way to go, Scoob!" Shaggy cheered, as he jumped onto the broken piece right behind Scooby-Doo. When they hit the mountainside, the piece served as a big snowboard.

"Let's shred this mountain before it shreds

us!" Shaggy shouted. Scooby-Doo and Shaggy snowboarded along the winding trail that Velma and Del had made for them. "All right, Scoob!" Shaggy said, laughing. "Who knew you were such a hotdog?"

Scooby-Doo pumped his fist happily.

Slowly, Scooby-Doo and Shaggy stopped smiling. They were nearly to the bottom but they were going too fast to stop! "I hate to be a backseat boarder, but what happens when we run out of mountain?" Shaggy asked nervously.

But Fred and the Gang had it all planned out. The path in the slope led right into the monastery. Scooby-Doo and Shaggy were thrown safely into a large snowdrift outside the monastery's doors.

Professor Jeffries and the snowman came skidding down the mountain, too. Pemba and the High Lama opened the gate to let them slide inside the courtyard. A load of crystals from the exploded cart slid in right after them.

"It worked!" Del said. He and Velma were still sitting on Del's snowcat, on a path by the monastery gate.

They didn't notice a giant wave of sliding

snow crashing down the mountain. It was an avalanche that had been started by the blast of dynamite on the cart. At the last minute, they saw what was coming at them. Del gunned the snowcat's engine. "Hang on, Velma," he cried as he tried to race out of the snow's path.

"I'm hanging!" Velma shouted, holding onto him tightly. It didn't look like they would make it. From the corner of her eye, she noticed a gigantic creature racing toward them. It was the Abominable Snowman! What was it doing?

CRASH!

The wall of snow hit the snowcat! Just seconds before it did, the snowman grabbed Del in one hand and Velma in the other. They watched as the crashing snow threw the snowcat into the air. The avalanche continued to rumble down the mountain, taking the snowcat with it.

Velma didn't know how the Abominable Snowman had gotten clear of the avalanche so quickly. Then she realized — the snowman was floating in the air above the ground!

"A floating Abominable Snowman," Del

called to her from the creature's hand. "Now I've seen everything!"

"This is no snowman!" Velma stated. She squirmed around in the giant hand, stretching forward. She reached for the top of the monster's head, preparing to pull off the mask it was wearing.

Chapter 9

"Minga has been behind this monster mystery all along!" Velma told the others. All of them were now safely in the monastery. Minga had taken off the Abominable Snowman costume and sat beside her brother, looking down, ashamed.

Fred nodded. "She used the helium tanks from the weather station to fill her monster costume. That was how the Abominable Snowman was able to climb so easily."

"And that's also why the monster's footprints didn't sink so deeply into the snow," Velma added.

Minga lifted her head. "I'm very sorry," she said. "I didn't mean to hurt anyone — especially not you, Pemba."

"I don't understand," Pemba replied. "Why did you do it?"

Minga nodded toward Del. "All I really wanted was to listen to Del Chillman on the radio." She turned toward Del. "You see, I'm your number one fan. I'd heard you say on the radio that you had come to the mountains hoping to see the Abominable Snowman but that you no longer believed it was real. When I learned you were going to be leaving the mountain, I brought the snowman to life as a way of keeping you here."

"Like, that's why she was trying to scare us all," Shaggy realized. "She was trying to convince Del to stick around."

"As for Professor Jeffries, he was only using the legend of the Abominable Snowman to cover up his scheme," Velma added.

Professor Jeffries glared at her. "And I would have gotten away with it, too, if it weren't for you meddling kids and that mountain-climbing mutt, Scooby-Doo!" he grumbled.

Scooby-Doo seemed pleased. "Roo, me?" he asked with a grin.

"So, like, is the Abominable Snowman just a myth, after all?" Shaggy wanted to know.

Before anyone could answer, Alphonse LeFleur

burst into the room. Everyone gasped, shocked to see him. "No, my friends!" he declared. "The Abominable Snowman is real!" He told them an amazing story. As he fell from the icy cliff, the real Abominable Snowman had grabbed him. It had carried him to its cave and allowed him to rest there. When he had recovered, the Abominable Snowman brought him back to safe ground and left him there, unharmed. "I can remember nothing else," Alphonse LeFleur said, finishing his tale.

"Zoinks!" Shaggy cried. "I think you've remembered plenty!"

The High Lama spread his arms out wide. "The legend of the Abominable Snowman lives on," he declared. "It is as timeless as the mountains themselves."

While all eyes were on the High Lama, Minga spoke quietly to Del. "I'm so sorry for all the trouble I have caused."

Del smiled at her. "Gee, Minga, what you did is so romantic . . . in a kind of twisted way . . . which I like! I'm not sure where we go from here."

Daphne had been listening to them talk and leaned forward. "I have an idea," she said.

Once again, the Gang sat in a Paris café. They had returned to enjoy what was left of their vacation.

Minga and Del were with them. Del leaned close and spoke to Minga in his best radio voice. "*Ah, mon cherie amor!*"

Minga giggled. Del's French accent wasn't very good, but she didn't mind. "Oh, I am loving the Paris!" she cried happily.

Scooby-Doo and Shaggy were also in love. They loved all the great French food piled high in front of them.

"Where's Freddie?" Daphne asked Velma. "He was supposed to meet us here an hour ago."

Daphne's cell phone began to ring and she answered it. Fred was on the other end. "It's me," he said. "I'm in some kind of weird Amazonian jungle. Bugs are crawling all over me! I must have gotten on the wrong plane!"

Scooby-Doo knew what that meant. He hopped into the Mystery Machine parked nearby and sat behind the wheel. Daphne, Velma, and

Shaggy joined him inside. "Like, step on it, Scoob!" Shaggy told him. "Our next stop is the Amazon Jungle!"

Scooby-Doo grinned, ready for the next adventure. "Rooby-rooby-roo!" he shouted gleefully as he stepped on the gas.

The end.

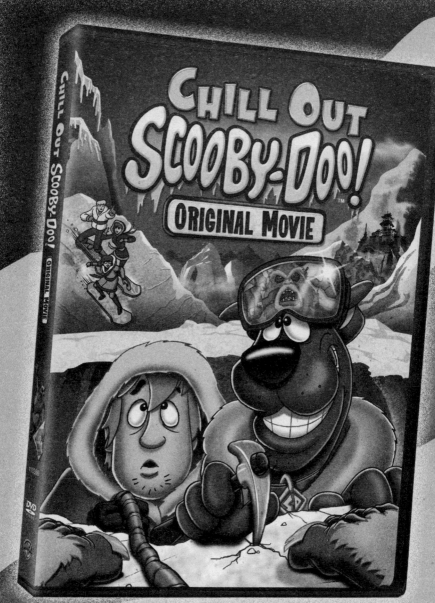

Available 9/4/07
on DVD!